Islamic Folklore

The Life of Prophet Syits AS (Seth)

Sons of Prophet Adam AS Bilingual Edition

by

Jannah Firdaus Mediapro

Muhammad Hamzah Sakura Ryuki

2023

Islamic Folklore The Life of Prophet Syits AS (Seth)
Sons of Prophet Adam AS Bilingual Edition

Jannah Firdaus Mediapro & Muhammad Hamzah Sakura Ryuki

Jannah Firdaus Mediapro

Publishing

2023

Islamic Folklore The Life of Prophet Syits AS (Seth)
Sons of Prophet Adam AS Bilingual Edition

Prologue

Islamic Folklore The Life of Prophet Syits AS (Seth) Sons of Prophet Adam AS Bilingual Edition In English Languange and German Languange. Based from The Noble Quran and Prophet Al-Hadist.

Prophet Syits AS (Seth) was born to Prophet Adam AS and Eve (Hawa), after Cain killed Abel. Allah SWT (God) gave the Revelation to Prophet Seth AS after the death of Prophet Adam AS. Allah SWT (God) revealed 50 booklets to Seth, as narrated by Ibn Hibban that Abu Dharr al-Ghifariyy heard this from Prophet Muhammad SAW.

Prophet Seth AS conveyed the message of Islam Faith to the people, telling the people the correct belief in Allah SWT (God) and the way to perform acceptable worship. All the humans were Muslim at that time, but still Allah SWT (God) gave the Revelation to Prophet Seth AS, and he taught and reminded the people.

Islamische Folklore Das Leben des Propheten Syits AS (Seth) Söhne des Propheten Adam AS Zweisprachige Ausgabe in englischer und deutscher Sprache. Basierend auf dem edlen Koran und Prophet Al-Hadist.

Prophet Syits AS (Seth) wurde dem Propheten Adam AS und Eva (Hawa) geboren, nachdem Kain Abel getötet hatte. Allah SWT (Gott) gab die Offenbarung an Prophet Seth AS nach dem Tod von Prophet Adam AS.

Allah, der Erhabene, offenbarte Seth 50 Broschüren, wie Ibn Hibban berichtet, dass Abu Dharr al-Ghifariyy dies vom Propheten Muhammad SAW gehört hat.

Prophet Seth AS überbrachte den Menschen die Botschaft des islamischen Glaubens, indem er ihnen den richtigen Glauben an Allah, den Erhabenen, und den Weg zu einem annehmbaren Gottesdienst erklärte. Alle Menschen waren zu dieser Zeit Muslime, aber dennoch gab Allah SWT (Gott) dem Propheten Seth AS die Offenbarung, und er lehrte und erinnerte die Menschen.

Chapter 1

Prophet Syits AS (Seth) was born to Prophet Adam AS and Eve (Hawa), after Cain killed Abel. Allah SWT (God) gave the Revelation to Prophet Seth AS after the death of Prophet Adam AS. Allah SWT (God) revealed 50 booklets to Seth, as narrated by Ibn Hibban that Abu Dharr al-Ghifariyy heard this from Prophet Muhammad SAW.

Prophet Seth AS conveyed the message of Islam Faith to the people, telling the people the correct belief in Allah SWT (God) and the way to perform acceptable worship. All the humans were Muslim at that time, but still Allah SWT (God) gave the Revelation to Prophet Seth AS, and he taught and reminded the people.

Prophet Seth AS received a new ruling from Allah SWT, different from the time of Prophet Adam AS. This ruling was that it is forbidden for the brother to marry his sister, whether she is his twin sister, or his sister who is not his twin.

Prophet Syits AS (Seth) wurde von Prophet Adam AS und Eva (Hawa) geboren, nachdem Kain Abel getötet hatte. Allah, der Erhabene, gab dem Propheten Seth AS nach dem Tod des Propheten Adam AS die Offenbarung. Allah, der Erhabene, offenbarte Seth 50 Broschüren, wie Ibn Hibban berichtet, dass Abu Dharr al-Ghifariyy dies vom Propheten Muhammad SAW gehört hat.

Prophet Seth AS überbrachte den Menschen die Botschaft des islamischen Glaubens, indem er ihnen den richtigen Glauben an Allah, den Erhabenen, und den Weg zu einem annehmbaren Gottesdienst erklärte. Alle Menschen waren zu dieser Zeit Muslime, aber dennoch gab Allah SWT (Gott) dem Propheten Seth AS die Offenbarung, und er lehrte und erinnerte die Menschen.

Prophet Seth AS erhielt von Allah, dem Erhabenen, eine neue Anordnung, die sich von der Zeit des Propheten Adam AS unterschied. Sie besagt, dass es dem Bruder verboten ist, seine Schwester zu heiraten, egal ob sie seine Zwillingsschwester ist oder seine Schwester, die nicht sein Zwilling ist.

Chapter 2

Prophet Adam AS was ill for eleven days before he died. Prophet Adam AS passed a will to his son Seth, ordering him to keep it sealed from Cain and Cain's son, due to their envy.

Prophet Seth AS lived in Makkah and performed Hajj and Umrah (a pilgrimage with some similarity to Hajj) and stayed there until he died.

Prophet Seth AS passed on the will to his child, Anush, and Anush passed the will to his son, Qaynan. Qaynan passed it to his son Mahlayil, and then to his son Yard, and then to his son Akhanukh, also known as Prophet Idris AS (Enoch).

Der Prophet Adam AS war elf Tage lang krank, bevor er starb. Prophet Adam AS hinterließ seinem Sohn Seth ein Testament, in dem er ihm auftrug, es vor Kain und Kains Sohn geheim zu halten, da diese neidisch seien.

Prophet Seth AS lebte in Mekka und verrichtete Hadsch und Umrah (eine Pilgerfahrt, die der Hadsch ähnelt) und blieb dort bis zu seinem Tod.

Prophet Seth AS vererbte das Testament an sein Kind Anusch, und Anusch gab das Testament an seinen Sohn Qaynan weiter. Qaynan gab es an seinen Sohn Mahlayil weiter, dann an dessen Sohn Yard und dann an dessen Sohn Akhanukh, der auch als Prophet Idris AS (Henoch) bekannt ist.

Chapter 3

According to the Book of Genesis, Prophet Seth AS was born when Prophet Adam AS was 130 years old (according to the Masoretic Text), or 230 years old (according to the Septuagint). The genealogy is repeated at 1 Chronicles 1:1–3. Genesis 5:4–5 states that Adam fathered "sons and daughters" before his death, aged 930 years. According to Genesis, Prophet Seth AS died at the age of 912.

In the Antiquities of the Jews, Josephus refers to Seth as virtuous and of excellent character, and reports that his descendants invented the wisdom of the heavenly bodies, and built the "pillars of the sons of Seth", two pillars inscribed with many scientific discoveries and inventions, notably in astronomy. They were built by Seth's descendants based on Adam's prediction that the world would be destroyed at one time by fire and another time by global flood, in order to protect the discoveries and be remembered after the destruction.

One was composed of brick, and the other of stone, so that if the pillar of brick should be destroyed, the pillar of stone would remain, both reporting the ancient discoveries, and informing men that a pillar of brick was also erected. Josephus reports that the pillar of stone remained in the land of Siriad in his day.

Although The Holy Quran makes no mention of Seth ibn Adam, he is revered within Islamic tradition as the third and righteous son of Adam and Eve and seen as the gift bestowed on Adam after the death of Abel. The Sunni scholar and historian ibn Kathir in his tarikh (book of history), Al-Bidaya wan nihaya records that Seth, a prophet like his father Adam, transfers God's Law to mankind after the death of Adam, and places him among the exalted antediluvian patriarchs of the Generations of Adam. Some sources say that Seth was the receiver of scriptures.

These scriptures are said to be the "first scriptures" mentioned in The Holy Quran 87:18. Medieval historian and exegete al-Tabari and other scholars say that Seth buried Adam and the secret texts in the tomb of Adam, i.e., the "Cave of Treasures".

The Islamic literature holds that Seth was born when Adam was past 100 and that Adam appointed Seth as guide to his people. The 11th-century Syrian historian and translator Al-Mubashshir ibn Fatik recorded the maxims and aphorisms of the ancient philosophers in his book Kitab mukhtār al-ḥikam wa-maḥāsin al-kalim and included a chapter on Seth.

Within Islamic tradition Seth holds wisdom of several kinds; knowledge of time, prophecy of the future Great Flood, and inspiration on the methods of night prayer.

Many traditional Islamic crafts are traced back to Seth, such as the making of horn combs. Seth also plays a role in Sufism, and Ibn Arabi includes a chapter in his Bezels of Wisdom on Seth, entitled "The Wisdom of Expiration in the Word of Seth" Nach dem Buch Genesis wurde der Prophet Seth AS geboren, als der Prophet Adam AS 130 Jahre alt war (nach dem masoretischen Text), oder 230 Jahre alt (nach der Septuaginta). Die Genealogie wird in 1 Chronik 1:1-3 wiederholt. In Genesis 5,4-5 heißt es, dass Adam "Söhne und Töchter" zeugte, bevor er im Alter von 930 Jahren starb. Nach der Genesis starb der Prophet Seth AS im Alter von 912 Jahren.

In den Altertümern der Juden bezeichnet Josephus Seth als tugendhaft und von ausgezeichnetem Charakter und berichtet, dass seine Nachkommen die Weisheit der Himmelskörper erfanden und die "Säulen der Söhne Seths" errichteten, zwei Säulen mit vielen wissenschaftlichen Entdeckungen und Erfindungen, vor allem in der Astronomie. Sie wurden von Seths Nachkommen auf der Grundlage von Adams Vorhersage, dass die Welt einmal durch Feuer und ein anderes Mal durch eine globale Flut zerstört werden würde, errichtet, um die Entdeckungen zu schützen und nach der Zerstörung in Erinnerung zu bleiben.

Die eine Säule bestand aus Ziegeln, die andere aus Stein, so dass im Falle der Zerstörung der Säule aus Ziegeln die Säule aus Stein erhalten blieb, die sowohl von den alten Entdeckungen berichtete als auch die Menschen darüber informierte, dass auch eine Säule aus Ziegeln errichtet worden war. Josephus berichtet, dass die Steinsäule zu seiner Zeit im Land Siriad erhalten blieb.

Obwohl der Heilige Koran keine Erwähnung von Seth ibn Adam enthält, wird er in der islamischen Tradition als dritter und rechtschaffener Sohn von Adam und Eva verehrt und als das Geschenk angesehen, das Adam nach dem Tod von Abel erhielt.

Der sunnitische Gelehrte und Historiker ibn Kathir schreibt in seinem Tarikh (Geschichtsbuch) Al-Bidaya wan nihaya, dass Seth, ein Prophet wie sein Vater Adam, nach dem Tod Adams das Gesetz Gottes an die Menschheit weitergibt, und zählt ihn zu den erhabenen antediluvianischen Patriarchen der Generationen Adams. In einigen Quellen heißt es, dass Seth der Empfänger der heiligen Schriften war.

Diese Schriften sollen die "ersten Schriften" sein, die im Heiligen Koran 87:18 erwähnt werden. Der mittelalterliche Historiker und Exeget al-Tabari und andere Gelehrte sagen, dass Seth Adam und die geheimen Texte in der Grabstätte Adams, d. h. in der "Höhle der Schätze", vergraben hat.

In der islamischen Literatur heißt es, dass Seth geboren wurde, als Adam über 100 Jahre alt war, und dass Adam Seth zum Führer seines Volkes ernannte. Der syrische Historiker und Übersetzer Al-Mubashshir ibn Fatik aus dem 11. Jahrhundert hat die Maximen und Aphorismen der alten Philosophen in seinem Buch Kitab mukhtār al-ḥikam wa-maḥāsin al-kalim aufgezeichnet und ein Kapitel über Seth aufgenommen.

In der islamischen Tradition besitzt Seth verschiedene Arten von Weisheit: Wissen über die Zeit, Prophezeiungen über die künftige Sintflut und Inspiration über die Methoden des Nachtgebets.

Viele traditionelle islamische Handwerke werden auf Seth zurückgeführt, wie z. B. die Herstellung von Hornkämmen. Seth spielt auch im Sufismus eine Rolle, und Ibn Arabi widmet Seth ein Kapitel in seinen "Bezels of Wisdom" mit dem Titel "The Wisdom of Expiration in the Word of Seth".

Chapter 4

From the words of Prophet Syits AS (Seth), son of Adam A believer must have sixteen qualities:

1- Getting to know God, His angels and people of obedience

2- Getting to know good and evil, that is, interest in good and keeping away from evil.

3- Listening to and obeying a merciful King whom God has made vicegerent on the earth giving him the affair of cities and servants.

4- Being kind to the parents.

5- Doing good to the extent of one's ability.

6- Helping the poor.

7- Being kind to the homeless.

8- Being brave in obeying Allah.

9- Keeping away from debauchery.

10- Patience with faith and certainty.

11- Truthfulness.

12- Justice.

13- Detachment from the world.

14- Making a sacrifice as a sing of thanks to God who has bestowed blessings upon His creatures.

15- Forbearance and thankfulness to God during calamities in the world without showing impatience.

16- Modesty and little disputation.

Aus den Worten des Propheten Syits AS (Seth), Sohn Adams Ein Gläubiger muss sechzehn Eigenschaften haben:

1- Kennenlernen von Gott, seinen Engeln und den Menschen, die gehorsam sind

2- Das Kennenlernen von Gut und Böse, d.h. das Interesse am Guten und das Fernhalten vom Bösen.

3- Auf einen barmherzigen König hören und ihm gehorchen, den Gott zu seinem Stellvertreter auf Erden gemacht hat, indem er ihm die Angelegenheiten der Städte und der Diener übertrug.

4- Den Eltern gegenüber freundlich sein.

5- Gutes zu tun, soweit man es kann.

6- Den Armen helfen.

7- Freundlich zu den Obdachlosen sein.

8- Mutig sein und Allah gehorchen.

9- Sich von Ausschweifungen fernhalten.

10- Geduld mit Glauben und Gewissheit.

11- Wahrhaftigkeit.

12- Gerechtigkeit.

13- Losgelöstheit von der Welt.

14- Ein Opfer darbringen als Dank an Gott, der seine Geschöpfe mit Segnungen beschenkt hat.

15- Nachsicht und Dankbarkeit gegenüber Gott während des Unglücks in der Welt, ohne Ungeduld zu zeigen.

16- Bescheidenheit und wenig Zank.

Author Bio

"Indeed, those who have believed and done righteous deeds – their Lord will guide them because of their faith.

Beneath them rivers will flow in the Gardens of Pleasure.

Their call therein will be, 'Exalted are You, O Allah,' and their greeting therein will be, 'Peace.'

And the last of their call will be, 'Praise to Allah, Lord of the worlds!'"

(From The Holy Quran)

www.ingramcontent.com/pod-product-compliance
Lightning Source LLC
LaVergne TN
LVHW052233110526
838202LV00095B/201